THE MONSTER IN ROOM 202

by Justine Korman
illustrated by Michael Chesworth

Troll Associates

I really don't like science class in Room 202. And I really don't like my science teacher, Mr. Fogg.

Everybody calls him Mr. Frog, because all he cares about are frogs. Slimy, gross, green frogs— yech!

One day I got bored and drew a picture of Mr. Fogg as a frog. Everyone thought it was pretty funny.

Except Mr. Fogg.

"Well, Skip," he said. "I guess you and I will be spending recess together today."

Mr. Fogg made me clean out all the frog aquariums.

"Be very careful," he said. "Don't let any of the frogs escape. We wouldn't want them to get hurt."

I think Mr. Fogg likes his slimy frogs more than he likes people.

My mom says Mr. Fogg must be shy. She says sometimes shy people feel more comfortable around animals than people.

I just think Mr. Fogg is as cold as a frog. The only difference is, he isn't green.

I looked out the window of smelly Room 202. Everyone was having a great time at recess. And there I was, stuck with Mr. Fogg!

I was hoping I could find a way to sneak outside. But Mr. Fogg didn't let me out of his sight. He was working on some experiment while he ate his lunch.

Mr. Fogg wrote very neat notes in his notebook. Then he mixed a bunch of stinky chemicals together.

Mr. Fogg saw me looking at him. "I'm working on a formula to create a super frog," he said.
I didn't know what to say.

"Excuse me for a moment, Skip," Mr. Fogg said. "I need one more chemical from the storage room."

As soon as he left, I ran over to the window. I saw Kenny running to catch a high fly ball.

"Go, Kenny!" I called.

Just then I heard a noise from behind. One of the frogs had leaped out of its aquarium.

"Oh, no!" I said. I must have forgotten to put the lid back on!

The frog leaped clear across the lab table. Then it knocked Mr. Fogg's formula right into his coffee cup!

I lunged toward the frog, but it had already hopped out the door. I started after it, but just then Mr. Fogg came back into the room.

"Whoa there, Skip," said Mr. Fogg, as he sat down. "What's your hurry?"

Before I could say a single word, Mr. Fogg took a sip of his coffee!

At first nothing happened. Then Mr. Fogg's skin started turning a funny color, and he got a really weird look on his face. He started to say something, but all that came out was...

Mr. Fogg's face and hands turned slimy and green. His shoes fell off and his feet became wide and webbed.

Mr. Fogg was a big, green monster!

And I was in big, big trouble.

From the hallway I heard the escaped frog *ribbit*. Mr. Fogg gave a big *ribbit* back, then leaped over me and out the door.

Hop, hop, hop. *Ribbit, ribbit, ribbit.*

Mr. Fogg and the frog leaped down the hall. I ran after them as fast as I could.

The door to the playground area was open, and out they went.

The frog headed straight for a nice, muddy puddle. I grabbed him just before weird Wendy got him.

Mr. Fogg wasn't going to be so easy to catch. His super-frog legs were so long, he was taking humongous jumps across the baseball field.

Before I knew what was happening, the
whole school was playing a giant game of
leapfrog! Even Principal Waggles joined in!

Finally, the bell rang. Everyone lined up to go inside—everyone except Mr. Fogg. He was still hopping like crazy.

I thought about leaving him out there, but I didn't want to get him in trouble. And after all, it was my fault that he turned into a frog-monster.

But what could I do?

Then something truly strange happened. I remembered something from Mr. Fogg's science class.

"Many experiments can be reversed," Mr. Fogg had told us.

"Maybe I can reverse Mr. Fogg's super-frog experiment," I thought. It was certainly worth a try. Besides, I didn't want to spend the rest of the year with a teacher who said, *"Ribbit"* whenever someone asked him a question.

I held up the frog for Mr. Fogg to see.
"Ribbit!" the frog croaked.
Mr. Fogg rolled his beady eyes our way.
"Ribbit!" he croaked back.

I ran with the frog back into the school.
Mr. Fogg followed right behind us.

We leaped down the halls and back to Room 202. As soon as Mr. Fogg had safely hopped through the door, I locked us all in.

I looked through Mr. Fogg's notes, then started pouring the stinky chemicals into the beakers.

I hate to admit it, but it was actually kind of fun.

Before I finished, I heard a strange sound.

"*Rib*...What's going on?" Mr. Fogg said in a croaky voice.

"Mr. Fogg!" I shouted. "You're back!"

I never thought I'd be so glad to see my science teacher.

Mr. Fogg's skin is still sort of green. And he spends recess playing leapfrog. But now he and I spend a lot of time together in the lab, working on some really cool experiments.

I guess Mr. Fogg turned out to be a pretty good guy after all.

But I really don't recommend eating lunch with him.